Mysterious Journey

clash within

AF674305

Avishek Trivedi

BlueRose ONE.com
Stories Matter
NewDelhi • London

BLUEROSE PUBLISHERS
India | U.K.

BlueRose ONE.com
Stories Matter
NewDelhi • London

For permissions requests or inquiries regarding this publication, please contact:

BLUEROSE PUBLISHERS
www.BlueRoseONE.com
info@bluerosepublishers.com
+91 8882 898 898
+4407342408967

ISBN: 978-93-6783-965-2

Cover design: Yash Singhal
Typesetting: Namrata Saini

First Edition: February 2025

Preface

In the swirling vortex of India's vibrant cities, lies a hidden world of ancient secrets, mysterious energies, and untold stories. Kolkata, the City of Joy, stands as a testament to this enigmatic landscape, where the past and present converge in a kaleidoscope of color, sound, and emotion.

This novel is a journey into the heart of Kolkata, where Raju, stumble upon a hidden reality that threatens to upend their lives forever. As he navigate the city's hidden corners, crumbling architecture, and whispered legends, he discover that the line between reality and myth blurs.

Inspired by the city's rich cultural heritage and the resilience of its people, this story explores the universal themes of friendship, self-discovery, and the struggle between light and darkness.

Through the eyes of Raju, we experience the pulsing rhythm of Kolkata, its contradictions and paradoxes, and the transformative power of determination.

Join me on this captivating journey into the soul of Kolkata, where secrets await, mysteries unfold, and the boundaries of reality are tested.

Contents

CHAPTER 1

Midnight Encounter

Raju and Kunal navigated the narrow alleys of Kolkata, the streetlights casting long shadows behind them. It was past midnight, and the city was alive with a different kind of energy.

They had agreed to meet at the old clock tower, a landmark in the heart of the city. As they approached, a figure emerged from the darkness.

"Follow me," the figure said, without looking back.

Raju and Kunal exchanged a curious glance and trailed behind the mysterious figure. They wound through the streets, passing by sleeping vendors and closed shops.

The figure stopped at a nondescript door, producing a key to unlock it. "Inside," he gestured.

Raju hesitated, but Kunal's curiosity got the better of him. They stepped inside, finding themselves in a dimly lit room filled with strange artifacts and oddities.

The figure revealed himself as Kabir, a collector of rare and obscure items. "I have something to show you," he said, his eyes glinting with excitement.

As Kabir led them deeper into the room, Raju felt a shiver run down his spine. What had they gotten themselves into?

Kabir stopped in front of a large, ornate box. "This is it," he said, his voice low and mysterious. "The reason I called you here tonight."

Raju and Kunal exchanged a curious glance. "What is it?" Raju asked.

Kabir smiled. "A piece of Kolkata's hidden history. Something that could change the way you see this city forever."

Kunal's eyes lit up with excitement. "Open it," he urged.

Kabir hesitated for a moment, then lifted the lid. A faint hum filled the air, and a soft, blue light spilled out.

Raju and Kunal peered into the box, and what they saw took their breath away. Inside, nestled in a bed of velvet, lay an ancient map of Kolkata, yellowed with age and adorned with strange symbols.

"This is incredible," Raju whispered.

Kabir nodded. "It's a map of the city's hidden pathways and secrets. Passed down through generations of Kolkata's guardians."

Kunal's eyes sparkled with excitement. "What secrets?"

Kabir leaned in, a conspiratorial look on his face. "Secrets of the past, hidden in plain sight. Secrets that could change the course of history."

Raju felt a shiver run down his spine. What had they stumbled into?
Kabir's eyes gleamed with intensity. "I've been searching for this map my whole life. And now, I need your help to uncover its secrets."

Raju and Kunal exchanged a hesitant glance. They had stumbled into something much bigger than themselves.

"What do you need us to do?" Raju asked, his voice cautious.

Kabir handed them a small, intricately carved box. "Solve the puzzle inside. It will reveal the first location marked on the map."

Kunal took the box, his fingers tracing the intricate patterns. "What's the puzzle?"

Kabir smiled. "That's for you to figure out. But be warned, you're not the only ones searching for this. There are those who will stop at nothing to claim the secrets of the map for themselves."

Raju felt a surge of adrenaline. They had to solve the puzzle before it fell into the wrong hands.

As they left Kabir's lair, the streets of Kolkata seemed to whisper secrets in their ears. They knew they had to move fast, to unravel the mysteries of the map before it was too late.

The box felt heavy in Kunal's hands, the puzzle waiting to be solved. They quickened their pace, the city lights blurring around them.

What secrets lay hidden in the map? And who else was searching for them?

As they walked, the box seemed to grow heavier, the puzzle inside taunting them. Raju and Kunal exchanged a determined glance. They would solve it, no matter what.

They arrived at Raju's small apartment, a cozy nest above his family's sweet shop. The aroma of freshly baked rasgullas wafted up, mingling with the scent of old books and curiosity.

Kunal opened the box, revealing a complex web of symbols and patterns. Raju leaned in, his eyes scanning the puzzle.

"This is crazy," Kunal whispered. "How are we supposed to solve it?"

Raju's fingers traced the symbols. "I think I see a pattern. Let me try."

As Raju worked on the puzzle, Kunal paced the room, his mind racing. Who else was searching for the map? And what secrets lay hidden in its ancient lines?

Suddenly, Raju's eyes lit up. "I think I've got it!"

The room fell silent as Raju's fingers moved swiftly, solving the puzzle. The box opened with a small click, revealing a hidden compartment.

Inside, a small, rolled-up parchment waited. Kunal unrolled it, revealing a cryptic message:

"Where shadows dance, light reveals
The first step on the hidden path"

Raju and Kunal exchanged a thrilled glance. They had done it! But what did the message mean?

CHAPTER 2

The Hidden Path

Raju and Kunal pored over the cryptic message, trying to decipher its meaning. "Where shadows dance, light reveals" - what could it possibly mean?

As they pondered, the first light of dawn crept into the room, casting a warm glow over the puzzle. Suddenly, Kunal's eyes widened.

"I think I know what it means!" he exclaimed. "The shadows on the walls of the Victoria Memorial Hall - they change with the light, don't they?"

Raju's eyes lit up. "And the hall is famous for its intricate stone carvings... maybe there's a hidden message there?"

Without another word, they grabbed their bags and set out for the Victoria Memorial Hall, racing against time to uncover the next clue.

As they arrived, the hall's majestic architecture took their breath away. They hurried inside, scanning the walls for any sign of the hidden message.

And then, they saw it - a subtle change in the shadow patterns, revealing a hidden symbol.

"Look!" Raju whispered, his finger tracing the symbol. "It's the same symbol from the map!"

Kunal's eyes sparkled. "We're on the right path!"

But as they turned to leave, they noticed something - a figure watching them from the shadows.

The figure stepped forward, revealing a woman with piercing green eyes and long, curly brown hair. She wore a traditional Bengali saree, but her attire seemed out of place in the modern hall.

"Who are you?" Raju asked, his instincts on high alert.

"I am Maya," she replied, her voice husky. "And you, my friends, are meddling in things you don't understand."

Kunal stood tall. "We're just trying to uncover the truth about the map."

Maya's eyes seemed to bore into their souls. "The truth is not for the faint of heart. You have no idea what you're dealing with."

Raju felt a shiver run down his spine. "What do you mean?"

Maya glanced around cautiously before leaning in. "The map is just the beginning. There are forces at play, forces that will stop at nothing to claim its secrets."

Suddenly, the hall's lights flickered, and the air grew thick with an eerie energy. Raju and Kunal exchanged a nervous glance.

"What's happening?" Kunal whispered.

Maya's eyes locked onto something behind them. "We have to get out of here. Now."

As they turned to leave, Raju saw it - a dark shadow looming in the doorway, its presence seeming to fill the entire hall.

Raju's heart raced as Maya grabbed their arms, pulling them toward a side exit. "Come on!" she urged.

As they burst through the door, the shadowy figure loomed closer, its presence suffocating. Raju could feel its icy breath on the back of his neck.

They sprinted across the grounds, Maya leading the way. "What is that thing?" Kunal panted.

Maya didn't look back. "A guardian. A protector of the map's secrets."

Raju's eyes widened. "What secrets?"

Maya stopped at a small gate, hidden behind a row of trees. "Not here. Not now. Come."

She pushed them through the gate, and they found themselves in a narrow alleyway, lined with old buildings. Maya led them deeper into the alley, stopping at a nondescript door.

"Inside," she said, her eyes scanning the rooftops.

Raju and Kunal exchanged a hesitant glance, but Maya's urgency was infectious. They stepped inside, finding themselves in a cramped, dimly lit room.

Maya closed the door, her eyes locking onto theirs. "Listen carefully. The map is just the beginning. There are five paths, each leading to a piece of the truth. But you're not the only ones searching."

Raju's mind reeled. "What truth?"

Maya's voice dropped to a whisper. "The truth about Kolkata's past. Its present. And its future."

Kunal's eyes sparkled with excitement. "What do you mean? What's so special about Kolkata's past?"

Maya's gaze seemed to cloud over, as if memories were surfacing. "Kolkata holds secrets, secrets that could change the course of history. And you, my friends, have stumbled into the midst of it."

Raju's curiosity was piqued. "What secrets?"

Maya hesitated, glancing around the room nervously. "I've said too much already. You need to be careful. There are those who will stop at nothing to keep the truth hidden."

Suddenly, a faint noise echoed outside, like footsteps on the rooftop. Maya's eyes darted toward the ceiling.

"It's them," she whispered. "We have to leave. Now."

Raju and Kunal exchanged a fearful glance. Who was after them? And what did they want?

Maya pushed them toward a small door at the back of the room. "Go! Find the next path. And be careful."

As they emerged into the bright sunlight, Raju felt a sense of trepidation. What lay ahead? And who could they trust?

They found themselves in a labyrinthine market, the sounds and smells of the city enveloping them. Maya had vanished, leaving them with only a cryptic message: "Follow the scent of sandalwood."

Raju sniffed the air, trying to pick up the fragrance. Kunal followed close behind, his eyes scanning the crowded stalls.

As they navigated the market, the scent of sandalwood grew stronger, leading them to a small, unassuming shop. The sign above the door read "Mohan's Antiques."

Raju pushed open the door, revealing a dimly lit interior filled with dusty artifacts. An old man, Mohan, looked up from behind the counter.

"Welcome, young friends," he said, his eyes twinkling. "I've been expecting you."

Kunal's eyes narrowed. "Expecting us? How did you know we were coming?"

Mohan smiled. "Maya sent word. You're searching for the next path, aren't you?"

Raju nodded, his heart racing with excitement.

Mohan beckoned them closer. "I have something for you. A clue to the next path."

He handed them a small, intricately carved box. Raju opened it, revealing a delicate silver pendant in the shape of a lotus flower.

"What does it mean?" Kunal asked.

Mohan's eyes seemed to cloud over. "The lotus flower represents the journey of the soul. You must follow its path to uncover the truth."

CHAPTER 3

The Lotus Path

Raju and Kunal left Mohan's shop, the silver pendant clutched in Raju's hand. They navigated the winding streets, trying to decipher the clue.

"The journey of the soul," Kunal repeated. "What does it mean?"

Raju studied the pendant. "I think it's a metaphor. We need to follow the path of the lotus flower to find the next clue."

As they walked, they noticed a series of intricate stone carvings on the buildings, depicting the life cycle of the lotus flower.

"Look!" Kunal exclaimed. "The carvings are showing us the way!"

They followed the carvings, which led them to a serene lake on the outskirts of the city. A small boat awaited them, adorned with lotus flowers.

Raju hesitated. "Do we trust this?"

Kunal nodded. "We have to try."

As they pushed off from the shore, the boat glided across the lake, stopping at a secluded pavilion. Inside, a wise old man sat cross-legged, surrounded by candles and incense.

"Welcome, seekers," he said, his voice soothing. "I have been waiting for you. You have reached the midpoint of your journey. Now, you must face the darkness within."

Raju and Kunal exchanged a nervous glance. What lay ahead?

The old man handed them a small, ornate mirror. "Look into the glass, and confront your deepest fears."

Raju hesitated, but Kunal took the mirror, gazing into its depths. Suddenly, his eyes widened in terror.

"What do you see?" Raju asked, his voice trembling.

Kunal's voice was barely audible. "I see myself failing, losing everything I hold dear."

Raju took the mirror, steeling himself for what he might see. But instead of fear, he saw a vision of his past, a memory he thought he'd forgotten.

A childhood memory of his grandfather, a wise and kind man, who had told him stories of Kolkata's hidden paths.

The old man nodded. "The mirror shows us our true selves. Now, you must confront the shadows within."

As they left the pavilion, Raju realized that the journey was not just about uncovering secrets, but also about facing their own demons.

The boat carried them back to the shore, where a figure waited in the shadows.

"Maya," Raju whispered, surprised.

Maya stepped forward, her eyes gleaming. "Well done, my friends. You have passed the first test. But the journey is far from over."

She handed them a small, intricately carved box. "Solve the riddle inside, and you shall find the next path."

Raju and Kunal exchanged a determined glance. They were ready for whatever lay ahead.

CHAPTER 4

The Shadow Weaver

In a hidden corner of Kolkata, a young woman named Leela sat at her loom, weaving a intricate fabric of shadows and light. She was a master of the ancient art of shadow weaving, passed down through generations of women in her family.

As she worked, a messenger arrived with a cryptic note from Maya. Leela's eyes widened as she read the message.

"The seekers need my help," she whispered to herself.

Leela's fingers flew across the loom, weaving a new pattern into the fabric. Suddenly, the room was filled with a soft, ethereal glow.

Raju and Kunal appeared in the doorway, drawn by the light. Leela beckoned them closer.

"I have been expecting you," she said, her voice like a gentle breeze. "Maya sent me a message. You need my help to decipher the riddle in the box."

Raju handed her the box, and Leela's fingers danced across its surface, feeling the intricate carvings.

"This is an ancient language," she said, her eyes closed in concentration. "But I can weave the answer into the fabric."

As she worked, the room grew darker, the shadows deepening. Suddenly, the fabric burst into a kaleidoscope of colors, revealing a hidden message.

Leela smiled. "The answer is clear. But are you prepared for what lies ahead?"

Raju and Kunal exchanged a resolute glance. They were ready to face whatever challenges awaited them.
Leela's eyes seemed to bore into their souls. "The next path leads to the Heart of Kolkata, a place where the city's deepest secrets reside. But to reach it, you must navigate the Maze of Reflections."

Raju's curiosity was piqued. "What's the Maze of Reflections?"

Leela's fingers wove a new pattern into the fabric. "A labyrinth of mirrors, where your deepest fears and desires will be revealed. You must confront your own reflections to reach the Heart."

Kunal's eyes narrowed. "And what lies within the Heart?"

Leela's smile was enigmatic. "The truth about Kolkata's past, and the source of its power. But be warned, the Heart is guarded by the Keeper of Secrets."

Raju's determination grew. "We're ready. Lead us to the Maze."

Leela nodded, her eyes glinting in the dim light. "Follow the fabric's pattern, and it will guide you through the Maze."

With that, she handed them a small, intricately woven cloth. Raju and Kunal took a deep breath, steeling themselves for the challenges ahead.

As they left Leela's lair, they felt the fabric's threads vibrating in their hands, leading them toward the Maze of Reflections.

They navigated the winding streets, following the fabric's subtle vibrations. The air grew thick with an eerie, pulsating mist, and the buildings seemed to twist and writhe around them.

Suddenly, they stumbled into a vast, dimly lit chamber filled with rows of ancient mirrors. The Maze of Reflections.

Raju's eyes widened as he gazed into the nearest mirror. His reflection stared back, distorted, revealing a deep-seated fear he'd never acknowledged.

Kunal's voice echoed through the chamber, his own reflection revealing a hidden desire.

As they navigated the maze, their reflections revealed secrets, fears, and desires they'd never confronted. The mirrors seemed to stretch on forever, each one revealing a new aspect of themselves.

But with every step, the reflections grew more distorted, the shadows deepening. Raju and Kunal realized they were not alone in the maze.

A figure emerged from the shadows - the Keeper of Secrets.

"You have reached the Heart of Kolkata," the Keeper intoned, its voice like a thousand whispers. "But to claim its secrets, you must first confront your own darkness."

Raju and Kunal steeled themselves, ready to face whatever lay within.

The Keeper of Secrets led them through the winding mirrors, into the Heart of Kolkata. They found themselves in a vast, underground chamber filled with ancient artifacts and strange devices.

Raju's eyes widened as he recognized a centuries-old map of Kolkata's hidden waterways. "This is the original plan for the city's canal system!"

Kunal marveled at a collection of antique scrolls. "These are ancient texts on Bengali mysticism!"

The Keeper spoke, its voice echoing off the walls. "Kolkata's secrets are not just historical, but mystical. The city's founders wove a web of energies, channeling the Ganges' power into its streets."

As they explored the Heart, they discovered hidden symbols etched into the walls - the same symbols they'd seen on the map.

Raju's mind raced. "This is it! The secrets of Kolkata's hidden paths!"

But the Keeper's next words chilled them. "You have uncovered the city's secrets, but now you must face the darkness that lies within its heart."

Suddenly, the chamber began to shake, and the symbols on the walls pulsed with a malevolent energy.

The ground trembled, and the air grew thick with an eerie, pungent scent. Raju and Kunal stumbled, disoriented, as the symbols on the walls blazed with an otherworldly light.

The Keeper's voice boomed, "The darkness within Kolkata's heart awakens! You must confront it to claim the city's secrets!"

A figure emerged from the shadows - a dark, twisted version of Kolkata's founder, Job Charnock.

Raju and Kunal stood frozen as the dark figure began to speak, its voice a malevolent echo of Charnock's. "I am the shadow of Kolkata's past, forged from the city's darkest secrets and desires."

The figure began to grow, its presence filling the chamber. Raju and Kunal knew they had to act fast.

With a surge of adrenaline, Raju grabbed the map, and Kunal seized the scrolls. Together, they channeled the knowledge of Kolkata's hidden paths and mystical energies against the darkness.

The air erupted in a blinding flash of light, and the chamber shook with a deafening roar. When the dust settled, the dark figure was gone, and the symbols on the walls pulsed with a newfound, benevolent energy.

The Keeper spoke, its voice filled with a sense of pride. "You have faced the darkness within Kolkata's heart and emerged victorious. The city's secrets are now yours to wield."

Raju and Kunal stood, exhausted but triumphant, as the Keeper handed them a small, ornate key. "This will unlock the doors to Kolkata's hidden paths. Use the city's secrets wisely."

CHAPTER 5

The Hidden Paths Unveiled

With the key in hand, Raju and Kunal left the Heart of Kolkata, ready to explore the city's hidden paths. They walked through the winding streets, the key glowing with a soft, blue light.

As they approached a nondescript wall, the key pulsed brighter. Raju inserted the key into a hidden lock, and a section of the wall slid open, revealing a narrow passageway.

They stepped into the passage, finding themselves in a labyrinthine network of tunnels and corridors. The air was thick with the scent of old books and forgotten memories.

Kunal's eyes sparkled. "This is incredible! The hidden paths are real!"

Raju grinned. "And we have the key to unlock them all!"

As they explored the passages, they stumbled upon hidden libraries, secret gardens, and ancient temples. Each new discovery filled them with wonder and awe.

But they soon realized they were not alone. A figure followed them, always lurking in the shadows.

Raju and Kunal exchanged a nervous glance. Who was this mysterious figure, and what did they want?

As they delved deeper into the passages, the figure drew closer, its presence more pronounced. Raju and Kunal quickened their pace, but the figure kept pace with them.

Suddenly, it stepped into the light, revealing a woman with piercing green eyes and long, curly brown hair. She wore a mischievous grin, and a hint of familiarity lingered in her features.

"Who are you?" Raju demanded, trying to hide his unease.

"I am Kamala," she replied, her voice husky. "A fellow seeker of Kolkata's secrets. And a friend of Maya's."

Kunal's eyes narrowed. "What do you want?"

Kamala chuckled. "Oh, I think you know. I want to join forces, to explore the hidden paths together. And uncover the secrets that lie within."

Raju and Kunal exchanged a skeptical glance. Could they trust this mysterious woman?

But Kamala's enthusiasm was infectious, and soon they found themselves walking together, exploring the hidden paths as a trio.

As they ventured deeper, the passages grew stranger, filled with ancient artifacts and mysterious symbols. Raju, Kunal, and Kamala realized they were unraveling a hidden narrative, one that threatened to upend everything they thought they knew about Kolkata.

As they explored further, they stumbled upon an ancient text etched into the walls. Kamala's eyes widened as she deciphered the script.

"This is the Chronicle of Kolkata," she breathed. "A lost history of the city's founders and their mystical practices."

Raju's curiosity was piqued. "What does it say?"

Kamala's voice trembled as she read aloud. "The founders made a pact with ancient powers, trading secrets and knowledge for the city's prosperity."

Kunal's eyes sparkled. "This is incredible! The secrets we've been searching for are right here."

But as they delved deeper into the chronicle, they realized that the pact came with a terrible cost. The city's prosperity was built on a dark foundation, one that threatened to consume everything. Raju's face set in determination. "We have to expose the truth. We can't let the city's secrets remain hidden."

Kamala nodded, her grin mischievous. "I knew you two were the right partners for this adventure."

Together, they vowed to unravel the mysteries of Kolkata's hidden paths, no matter the danger. Little did they know, their actions would set off a chain reaction, awakening forces that had lain dormant for centuries.

CHAPTER 6

The Shadows Stir

As they left the hidden passages, Raju, Kunal, and Kamala couldn't shake off the feeling that they were being watched. The streets seemed to grow darker, the shadows twisting into menacing forms.

Kamala glanced over her shoulder. "We've disturbed something. The city's secrets don't want to be exposed."

Raju quickened his pace. "We need to get the chronicle to Maya. She'll know what to do."

But as they approached Maya's shop, they found it in disarray. Books scattered everywhere, and the air was thick with the scent of sandalwood and smoke.

Maya emerged from the shadows, her eyes blazing. "You've unleashed a storm. The city's hidden forces won't let us expose the truth without a fight."

Kunal stood tall. "We won't back down. We have to reveal the secrets."

Maya's gaze fell upon Kamala. "You've brought a wild card into this. Her motives are unclear."

Kamala's smile was enigmatic. "My motives are pure. I want the truth revealed, no matter the cost."

As tensions rose, the shadows in the room began to stir, taking on a life of their own. Raju, Kunal, and Kamala realized they were surrounded by forces beyond their control.

The shadows coalesced into dark, humanoid figures that closed in on the group. Maya raised her hands, and the air was filled with the scent of sandalwood and smoke as she chanted an ancient incantation.

The figures halted, but their presence seemed to grow more menacing. Kamala stepped forward, her eyes flashing with a fierce inner light.

"I can handle this," she said, her voice low and mysterious.

With a swift gesture, she summoned a whirlwind of colorful silks that enveloped the dark figures. The shadows let out a collective hiss as they were repelled by the vibrant fabrics.

Raju and Kunal watched in awe as Kamala expertly wielded the silks, using them to bind and banish the shadowy entities.

Maya nodded in approval. "You have skills, Kamala. But we can't keep running. We need a plan to expose the truth and bring the hidden forces to light."

Kamala's smile was enigmatic. "I have a plan. But it requires trust and courage."

Raju and Kunal exchanged a glance. They had come too far to turn back now.

"We're in," Raju said, his voice firm.

Kunal nodded. "Together, we'll uncover the secrets of Kolkata."

Kamala's eyes gleamed with a fierce light. "Then let's begin."

CHAPTER 7

The Plan Unfolds

Kamala led them to a hidden courtyard deep in the heart of Kolkata. The air was thick with the scent of blooming flowers and the sound of soft chanting.

"Welcome to the Heart of the City," Kamala said, her eyes shining with a deep connection to the place. "Here, we will weave a new narrative for Kolkata, one that reveals the truth and brings the hidden forces to light."

Maya nodded, her hands weaving intricate patterns in the air. "We will use the Chronicle of Kolkata as the foundation, and Kamala's silks as the threads to bind the story together."

Raju's mind raced with the possibilities. "And how do we share this new narrative with the world?"

Kamala's smile was mischievous. "Leave that to me. I have a plan to weave the story into the fabric of the city itself."

As they worked, the courtyard began to transform. Colors danced across the walls, and the air vibrated with an otherworldly energy.

Kunal's eyes widened in wonder. "We're creating something incredible here."

Maya's voice was filled with a deep wisdom. "We are not just creating a story, we are reshaping the destiny of Kolkata."

But as the plan unfolded, a dark presence watched from the shadows, waiting for its moment to strike.

As the night wore on, the courtyard transformed into a vibrant tapestry of colors and patterns. Kamala's silks seemed to come alive, weaving a narrative that pulsed with the city's rhythm.

Raju felt the energy building, as if the very fabric of Kolkata was being rewoven. "It's working," he whispered, his eyes locked on the swirling colors.

Kunal nodded, his face aglow with wonder. "The city is responding to our story."

Maya's hands moved with a newfound urgency, as if she sensed the darkness gathering at the edges. "We must complete the narrative before the shadow forces intervene."

Kamala's voice rose above the chanting. "The final thread must be woven with courage and conviction."

As she spoke, a figure emerged from the shadows - a figure with eyes that burned like embers from the underworld.

"You dare to challenge the hidden forces?" it growled, its voice like thunder in the courtyard.

Raju, Kunal, and Maya stood firm, their hearts pounding in unison. Kamala raised her hands, and the silks responded, weaving a shield of light around them.

"We will not be silenced," Kamala declared, her voice ringing through the courtyard. "The truth of Kolkata will be told."

The figure sneered, its presence growing darker, more menacing. "Then let the shadows speak."

The figure raised its hand, and the shadows around it began to twist and writhe like living serpents. The air grew colder, heavy with malevolent energy.

Kamala's shield of light trembled, but she stood firm, her eyes flashing with defiance. Raju, Kunal, and Maya stood shoulder to shoulder, their hearts pounding in unison.

The figure began to chant, its voice dripping with malice. The shadows grew longer, darker, and more menacing, as if they were being summoned from the very depths of the underworld.

Suddenly, the lights in the courtyard flickered and died, plunging them into darkness. The only sound was the soft whisper of the shadows, growing louder, closer...

Raju felt a cold breath on the back of his neck, making his skin crawl. Kunal's hand grasped his, a silent signal of solidarity. Maya's eyes glowed like embers in the dark, her presence a beacon of hope.

Kamala's voice cut through the darkness, her words a fierce battle cry. "We will not be consumed! The truth of Kolkata will prevail!"

But as she spoke, the shadows seemed to coalesce into a single, dark entity, its presence overwhelming, crushing...

And then, everything went black.

CHAPTER 8

The Darkness Recedes

Raju's eyes fluttered open, his mind foggy. He was lying on the courtyard floor, his head throbbing. Kunal and Maya were beside him, their faces etched with concern.

Kamala stood over them, her eyes blazing with a fierce inner light. "The shadows have receded," she said, her voice husky. "But the darkness will return. We must complete the narrative."

Raju struggled to his feet, his mind racing. "What happened?"

Kunal helped Maya up. "The shadows overwhelmed us. But Kamala's silks... they protected us."

Maya's eyes locked onto Kamala. "Your fabrics hold more power than we realized."

Kamala's smile was enigmatic. "The silks are merely a conduit. The true power lies within the narrative."

As they spoke, the courtyard began to transform. The colors returned, vibrant and alive. The air vibrated with energy.

Raju's eyes widened. "The narrative is changing. It's adapting to the darkness."

Kamala nodded. "The story is becoming stronger. But we must finish it. Now."

With renewed urgency, they worked, their hands moving in tandem as they wove the final threads of the narrative.

But as they worked, a faint whisper echoed through the courtyard, a soft warning: "The darkness will not be defeated so easily..."

CHAPTER 9

The Hidden Thread

As they finished the narrative, a sudden stillness fell over the courtyard. The colors dimmed, and the air grew heavy with anticipation.

Kamala's eyes gleamed with a knowing light. "The story is complete. But there is one final thread to weave."

Raju's curiosity was piqued. "What thread?"

Kamala's smile was enigmatic. "The thread of the unknown. The hidden pattern that binds the narrative together."

Maya's eyes narrowed. "I sense it too. A presence, lurking just beyond the edge of perception."

Kunal's voice was barely above a whisper. "What if it's not just a thread? What if it's a doorway?"

As they spoke, the air seemed to vibrate with an otherworldly energy. The colors in the courtyard began to shift, revealing a hidden pattern that had been there all along.

Raju's mind raced. "This changes everything. The narrative is more than just a story. It's a key."

Kamala's eyes locked onto his. "A key to what?"

Raju's voice was filled with wonder. "To the secrets of Kolkata itself. To the mysteries that lie beyond the veil."

As they gazed upon the hidden pattern, the courtyard began to fade away, revealing a glimpse of a world beyond their wildest dreams.

The vision vanished as suddenly as it appeared, leaving them stunned and bewildered. Kamala's eyes gleamed with an inner light, as if she saw beyond the veil.

Raju's mind reeled with questions. "What lies beyond? What secrets does the narrative hold?"

Kamala's smile was enigmatic. "The thread of the unknown is a doorway to the hidden heart of Kolkata. Are you prepared to step through?"

Maya's voice was laced with trepidation. "We don't know what lies beyond. We can't just step into the unknown."

Kamala's gaze fell upon Maya. "You've always sensed the mysteries of the city. Now's the chance to uncover them."

Kunal's eyes sparkled with adventure. "We've come this far. Let's see where the thread leads."

Raju nodded, his heart pounding with excitement. "Together, we'll uncover the secrets of Kolkata."

With Kamala leading, they stepped forward, into the unknown. The courtyard dissolved, replaced by a labyrinthine passage that stretched into the heart of the city.

As they walked, the air thickened with anticipation. They sensed they were being drawn into a world where myth and reality blurred.

Suddenly, the passage opened into a vast underground chamber, filled with ancient artifacts and mysterious symbols.

Kamala's voice whispered in awe. "The hidden heart of Kolkata. Here lies the city's deepest secret."

The chamber was a treasure trove of ancient relics and mysterious artifacts. Raju's eyes widened as he took in the sight of glowing orbs, ancient texts, and strange devices.

Maya's voice was barely above a whisper. "This is incredible. The secrets of Kolkata are laid bare before us."

Kamala's eyes shone with a deep understanding. "This is the heart of the city, where the ancient ones once walked."

Kunal's curiosity got the better of him. "What are these devices? They look like some sort of technology."

Kamala's smile was enigmatic. "They are keys to unlocking the city's true potential. The ancient ones knew secrets we can only dream of."

Raju's mind raced with questions. "What secrets? What potential?"

Kamala's gaze fell upon him. "The secrets of time and space. The potential to bend reality itself."

As they explored the chamber, they stumbled upon an ancient text, bound in a strange, glowing material.

Maya's eyes widened as she opened the book. "This is it. The Chronicle of Kolkata. The secrets of the city are here."

But as they delved deeper into the text, they realized that the secrets came with a warning: "Beware the guardians of the city. They will stop at nothing to keep the secrets buried."

CHAPTER 10

The Guardians of the City

As they read on, the air in the chamber began to shift, and the shadows seemed to grow longer. Kamala's eyes gleamed with a knowing light.

"The guardians are stirring," she whispered. "We must be careful."

Raju's heart quickened. "What do we do?"

Kamala's smile was enigmatic. "We must solve the riddle of the chronicle. It holds the key to unlocking the secrets of the city."

Maya's eyes scanned the text. "I think I've found it. A riddle that speaks of the city's heart."

Kunal's voice was filled with excitement. "Let's solve it! We can't let the guardians catch us."

As they worked on the riddle, the chamber grew darker, and the shadows seemed to twist and writhe like living things.

Suddenly, the air was filled with a low, ominous hum. The guardians had arrived.

Kamala's eyes flashed with a fierce inner light. "We must leave now! The guardians will not hesitate to strike."

But as they turned to flee, they found themselves face to face with the guardians of the city - towering figures with eyes that burned like stars.

The guardians loomed before them, their eyes blazing with an otherworldly intensity. Raju felt a shiver run down his spine as Kamala stepped forward, her hands weaving intricate patterns in the air.

"We mean no harm," she said, her voice steady. "We seek only to unlock the secrets of the city."

The guardians regarded her for a moment, then spoke in unison, their voices like thunder. "You have disturbed the balance. You must pay the price."

Maya stepped forward, her eyes flashing with defiance. "We won't back down. We have the right to know the truth."

The guardians raised their hands, and the air seemed to thicken, as if reality itself was bending to their will. Kunal felt a strange sensation, as if he was being pulled apart and put back together again.

Raju's vision blurred, and when it cleared, he saw that the guardians had vanished. But in their place stood a figure he knew all too well - the enigmatic stranger from the streets of Kolkata.

"Welcome, Raju," the stranger said, with a hint of a smile. "I see you're determined to uncover the secrets of the city. Very well, I shall show you."

And with that, the stranger reached out and touched Raju's forehead. The world around him dissolved into chaos, and Raju felt himself being pulled into a realm beyond his wildest dreams.

CHAPTER 11

The Realm Beyond

Raju's mind reeled as he stumbled through a realm that defied all logic. The stranger's touch had unlocked a doorway to a world beyond the veil of reality.

Colors swirled around him, like a mad artist's palette. Shapes twisted and writhed, like living things. The air was filled with a cacophony of sounds, each one more jarring than the last.

The stranger's voice whispered in his ear, guiding him through the chaos. "This is the realm of the city's heart. Here, the secrets of Kolkata await."

Raju's eyes adjusted slowly to the madness around him. He saw visions of the city's past, present, and future. He saw the threads that connected every moment, every decision, every life.

The stranger led him to a great crystal, pulsing with an inner light. "This is the heart of Kolkata," the stranger said. "Here lies the source of the city's power."

Raju reached out a trembling hand, feeling the energy coursing through the crystal. Suddenly, visions flooded his mind - the secrets of the city, the mysteries of the universe.

He saw the truth of the chronicle, the purpose of the guardians, and the destiny of the city. He saw the threads that connected him to Maya, Kunal, and Kamala.

The stranger's voice whispered once more, "Now you know the secrets of Kolkata. Will you use this knowledge to shape the city's future, or will you succumb to its power?"

Raju's mind reeled, struggling to comprehend the weight of the secrets he now held. The fate of Kolkata hung in the balance, and he was the key.

CHAPTER 12

The Choice

Raju's eyes snapped open, and he found himself back in the chamber, surrounded by his friends. The stranger was nowhere to be seen, but the memories of the realm beyond lingered.

Maya's eyes searched his face. "Raju, what happened? You were gone for hours."

Raju's mind raced, trying to process the secrets he had uncovered. "I saw the heart of Kolkata," he said, his voice barely above a whisper. "I know the truth."

Kunal's eyes lit up with excitement. "What is it? Tell us!"

Raju hesitated, unsure if he should reveal the secrets he had learned. But something about his friends' eager faces made him trust them.

"The chronicle is more than just a story," he began. "It's a key to unlocking the city's true potential. And we're the ones who can do it."

Kamala's eyes gleamed with understanding. "We have the power to shape the city's future."

Maya's voice was filled with determination. "Then let's do it. Let's unlock the secrets of Kolkata and create a new destiny."

But as they nodded in agreement, Raju felt a shadowy presence watching them from the shadows. The guardians had not forgotten, and they would stop at nothing to keep the secrets buried.

Raju's heart raced as he realized the weight of their decision. They were choosing to defy the guardians and unlock the secrets of Kolkata.

"We must be careful," Kamala warned, her eyes scanning the shadows. "The guardians will not hesitate to strike."

Maya's voice was filled with determination. "We can't let fear stop us. We have the power to create a new future."

Kunal nodded in agreement. "Together, we can do this."

Raju took a deep breath, steeling himself for what lay ahead. "Then let's begin. Let's unlock the secrets of Kolkata and shape the city's destiny."

As they spoke, the chamber began to glow with a soft, pulsing light. The air vibrated with energy, and the shadows seemed to recoil.

The guardians emerged from the darkness, their eyes blazing with fury. "You dare to defy us?" they thundered.

Raju stood tall, his heart pounding in his chest. "We dare to create a new future. A future where Kolkata's secrets are used for the greater good."

The guardians snarled, their forms blurring as they prepared to strike. But Raju and his friends stood firm, ready to face whatever lay ahead.

The fate of Kolkata hung in the balance, and they were the ones who would tip the scales.

CHAPTER 13

The Confrontation

The guardians unleashed a torrent of energy, but Raju and his friends stood firm, their bond and determination shielding them from the attack. Kamala's hands wove intricate patterns, deflecting the guardians' blows. Maya's voice rang out, her words imbuing the air with a powerful resonance. Kunal's eyes blazed with a fierce inner light, his presence anchoring the group.

Raju faced the guardians, his heart filled with a sense of purpose. "We won't back down," he declared. "We'll unlock the secrets of Kolkata and create a brighter future."

The guardians snarled, their forms shifting and flowing like molten lava. But Raju's friends stood firm, their combined energy creating a barrier against the guardians' fury.

Slowly, the guardians began to falter, their power waning as Raju's friends continued to defy them. The chamber's energy reached a fever pitch, the air vibrating with anticipation.

In a final, desperate bid to stop them, the guardians merged into a single, colossal entity. The creature's eyes blazed with fury as it unleashed a devastating blast of energy.

Raju's friends stumbled back, their bond strained to the breaking point. But Raju stood firm, his heart filled with a fierce determination. With a cry of triumph, he reached out and touched the creature's heart.

The guardians' energy dissipated, their forms dissipating like mist in the sun. The chamber fell silent, the only sound the heavy breathing of Raju and his friends.

They had done it. They had unlocked the secrets of Kolkata and claimed the city's destiny as their own.

But as they stood victorious, a new presence emerged from the shadows. A figure with eyes that shone like stars and skin as white as marble.

"Congratulations, Raju," the figure said, its voice like music. "You have unlocked the secrets of Kolkata. But do you have the wisdom to wield its power?"

CHAPTER 14

The New Guardian

The figure stepped forward, its presence radiating an otherworldly grace. Raju felt a sense of awe wash over him as he realized that this being was the true guardian of Kolkata's secrets.

"Who are you?" Raju asked, his voice barely above a whisper.

"I am the Keeper of the City's Heart," the being replied, its voice like a gentle breeze. "And you, Raju, are the chosen one, destined to wield the power of Kolkata's secrets."

Raju's mind reeled as the Keeper began to explain the true nature of the city's power. "Kolkata's secrets are not just a collection of knowledge, but a living, breathing entity that pulses with the energy of the city itself."

Maya's eyes widened in wonder. "That's what we felt in the chamber! The city's energy coursing through us!"

The Keeper nodded. "You have been chosen to harness this energy, to wield the power of Kolkata's secrets for the greater good."

Kunal's voice was filled with excitement. "What does this mean? What can we do with this power?"

The Keeper's smile was enigmatic. "The possibilities are endless. You can reshape the city, mold its destiny, and create a brighter future for all its inhabitants."

Raju felt a sense of trepidation mixed with excitement. He knew that this power came with great responsibility, and he was determined to use it wisely.

As the Keeper vanished into the shadows, Raju and his friends shared a look of determination. They knew that their journey was far from over, but they were ready to face whatever lay ahead, armed with the power of Kolkata's secrets.

CHAPTER 15

The New Era

With the power of Kolkata's secrets coursing through them, Raju and his friends set out to reshape the city's destiny. They started small, using their newfound abilities to help those in need.

Maya used her knowledge of the city's hidden patterns to navigate the streets and deliver aid to remote areas. Kunal employed his understanding of the city's energy to revitalize neglected neighborhoods. Kamala utilized her connection to the city's heart to heal the emotional wounds of its inhabitants.

Raju, with his deep understanding of the city's secrets, coordinated their efforts, ensuring that their individual actions harmonized to create a greater whole.

As they worked, the city began to transform. Neighborhoods once plagued by darkness and despair now flourished with light and hope. The streets, once filled with fear and uncertainty, became vibrant with life and possibility.

The people of Kolkata began to notice the change, and soon, they too joined in, contributing their own unique skills and talents to the transformation.

A new era dawned on Kolkata, one of hope and possibility. Raju and his friends had unlocked the secrets of the city, and in doing so, had unleashed a power that would forever change the face of the metropolis.

Years passed, and the city continued to evolve. Raju and his friends became legends, their names synonymous with bravery and wisdom. But they knew that the true hero was the city itself, its secrets and energy now harnessed for the greater good.

And so, they continued to watch over Kolkata, ever vigilant, always ready to defend the city against any threat that might arise. For they knew that the power of the city's secrets was not just a gift, but a responsibility to be wielded with care and wisdom.

But as the years passed, a subtle change crept over Raju. He began to realize that the power of Kolkata's secrets came with a terrible cost. The city's energy, once a vibrant and life-giving force, had become a constant whisper in his mind, urging him to use its power for his own gain.

Raju tried to resist, but the temptation grew stronger with each passing day. He started to use the city's secrets to manipulate events, to bend the world to his will. His friends, once his closest allies, grew wary of him, sensing the change in his heart.
And then, one fateful night, Raju vanished.

Maya, Kunal, and Kamala searched for him, but he was nowhere to be found. It was as if he had been consumed by the very power he once wielded.

The city, once a beacon of hope, began to crumble. The energy that had once flowed through its streets now seemed to pulse with a dark and malevolent force.

Raju's friends realized, too late, that the true secret of Kolkata was not its power, but its curse. The city's energy was never meant to be harnessed, only respected.

As they struggled to come to terms with their failure, a figure emerged from the shadows. Raju, his eyes now blazing with an otherworldly energy, revealed his true intentions.

"I am the master of Kolkata's secrets," he declared, his voice dripping with malevolence. "And I will use its power to reshape the world in my image."

The city trembled, its very foundations shaking with fear. For in that moment, Raju's friends knew that they had unleashed a terror beyond their wildest imagination.

CHAPTER 16

The Shadow of Raju

Maya, Kunal, and Kamala knew they had to act fast. They couldn't let Raju's darkness consume the city. They banded together, using their unique skills to try and stop him.

But Raju was too powerful. He had harnessed the full force of Kolkata's secrets, and his abilities were now rivalled only by the city itself.

As the battle raged on, the city began to tear itself apart. Buildings crumbled, streets cracked, and the skies grew dark.

In a last-ditch effort, Maya remembered the words of the Keeper: "The city's secrets are not just a collection of knowledge, but a living, breathing entity that pulses with the energy of the city itself."

She realized that the only way to stop Raju was to awaken the city's true power.

With newfound determination, Maya reached deep within herself and connected with the city's heart. The energy surged through her, and she became one with Kolkata.

Raju, sensing his control slipping, unleashed a devastating blast of energy. But Maya, now a vessel for the city's power, absorbed the attack and countered with a force that shook the very foundations of the metropolis.

Raju stumbled back, his eyes wide with shock. For the first time, he saw the true extent of his mistake.

The city, now fully awakened, began to purge itself of Raju's darkness. The energy that had once fueled his ambitions now turned against him.

As the shadows closed in, Raju realized too late that he had become the very evil he once sought to destroy.

And so, the city of Kolkata was reborn, its secrets and power once again in balance. But the memory of Raju's darkness would never be forgotten, a cautionary tale of the dangers of unchecked ambition.

CHAPTER 17

The Streets of Kolkata Reborn

As the city purged itself of Raju's darkness, the streets of Kolkata began to transform. The once-narrow alleys of the old town expanded, revealing hidden courtyards and secret gardens. The crumbling buildings of the colonial era were reborn, their facades gleaming with a newfound radiance.

The streets themselves seemed to come alive, as if the city's energy had infused them with a vibrant pulse. The pavement stones shimmered like diamonds, and the streetlights danced with a warm, golden glow.

In the heart of the city, the iconic Victoria Memorial gleamed like a beacon, its marble surfaces reflecting the colors of the rainbow. The nearby Maidan, once a dusty expanse, was now a lush oasis, its greenery stretching towards the sky like a canvas of emeralds.

In the north, the bustling streets of Shyambazar and Bagbazar were reborn, their markets overflowing with exotic spices, colorful fabrics, and sweet delicacies. The air was filled with the aroma of street food, and the sound of laughter and chatter.

In the south, the trendy boutiques and cafes of Park Street and Camac Street pulsed with a cosmopolitan vibe, attracting visitors from far and wide. The nearby Indian Museum, once a dusty relic, was now a state-of-the-art showcase of the city's rich cultural heritage.

As the city's transformation continued, its residents marveled at the beauty and magic that surrounded them. They knew that they owed it all to Maya, Kunal, and Kamala, who had saved Kolkata from the brink of destruction.

And so, the city's residents celebrated, their joy and gratitude echoing through the streets like a never-ending festival. For in Kolkata, the city of joy, the streets themselves had become a testament to the power of friendship and determination.

CHAPTER 18

The Legacy of the Four Friends

Years passed, and the legend of Maya, Kunal, Kamala, and Raju grew. The city's residents whispered stories of their bravery and selflessness, how they had saved Kolkata from destruction.

The four friends became icons, their names etched in the city's history. Maya's connection to the city's heart was celebrated, Kunal's strategic mind was revered, Kamala's compassion was admired, and Raju's cautionary tale was remembered.

As the city continued to thrive, a new generation emerged, inspired by the four friends' legacy. They formed their own groups, exploring the city's secrets and working together to build a better future.

The city's transformation had created new wonders, from the glowing street art of the old town to the vibrant cultural festivals that celebrated its diversity.

One day, a young girl named Aisha stumbled upon an ancient text hidden deep within the city's archives. It was the chronicle of the four friends, their journey, and their sacrifice.

Aisha felt an instant connection to their story and knew she had to share it with the world. She spent years researching, interviewing, and writing, determined to bring their legend to life.

And so, the story of Maya, Kunal, Kamala, and Raju was reborn, inspiring a new generation to explore, discover, and protect the city they loved.

The four friends' legacy lived on, a reminder that even in the darkest times, friendship, determination, and a willingness to learn from mistakes can lead to a brighter future.

CHAPTER 19

The Dream

Raju's eyes fluttered open, and he found himself on a crowded bus, rumbling through the streets of Kolkata. He rubbed his eyes, trying to shake off the vivid dream he had just had.

It had felt so real - the friends, the adventure, the battle to save the city. But it was just a dream, he told himself.

As he looked around at the familiar faces of the commuters, Raju couldn't shake off the feeling that something was off. The dream had felt too real, too vivid.

He thought back to the events of the dream, trying to make sense of it all. The friends, the secrets, the battle to save the city... it had all seemed so real.

And then, like a bolt of lightning, it hit him. The dream wasn't just a dream. It was a warning.

Raju's heart racing, he grabbed his bag and pushed his way through the crowded bus. He had to get off, had to clear his head.

As he emerged onto the bustling streets, Raju knew what he had to do. He had to find Maya, Kunal, and Kamala. He had to tell them about the dream, about the warning.

For Raju knew that the dream was more than just a dream. It was a call to action. A call to save the city, before it was too late.

And so, Raju set off on a new journey, one that would take him to the depths of Kolkata's secrets and back again. For he knew that the dream was just the beginning, and that the real adventure was only just starting.

CHAPTER 20

The Unraveling Mind

Raju's eyes scanned the familiar streets of Kolkata, but his mind played tricks on him. The buildings seemed to shift, the people blurred together, and the sounds echoed with an otherworldly quality.

He knew it was happening again – the illusions.

Raju's psychologist, Dr. Sen, had diagnosed him with schizophrenia, but Raju refused to accept it. He believed the city was speaking to him, guiding him through the labyrinthine streets.

As he walked, the illusions intensified. Maya, Kunal, and Kamala appeared beside him, their faces distorted, their voices whispering cryptic messages.

"Raju, we're not real," Maya's illusion whispered. "You're losing grip on reality."

Raju's grip on his backpack tightened. He knew the difference between reality and illusion – or so he thought.

Suddenly, the streets disappeared, replaced by a kaleidoscope of colors. Raju stumbled, disoriented.

A voice echoed in his mind – Dr. Sen's voice. "Raju, your medication..."

Raju's eyes snapped open. He stood in his small apartment, surrounded by scattered papers and broken pencils. The city outside seemed quiet, normal.

But Raju knew better. The illusions would return.

He scribbled furiously in his journal:

"I must hold on to reality. The city needs me. My friends need me."

As he wrote, the words blurred, and the paper ripped.

Raju's mind was unraveling.

CHAPTER 21

The Descent into Darkness

Raju's days blurred together – medication, therapy, and the constant battle against the illusions.

Dr. Sen increased the dosage, but Raju felt himself slipping further away.

One night, he woke up to find his apartment transformed. The walls were covered in ancient symbols, pulsing with an eerie glow.

Maya's illusion stood before him, her eyes black as coal. "Raju, come with me."

Raju's heart pounded. He knew he shouldn't trust the illusions, but...

He followed Maya's illusion into the heart of Kolkata.

The city was alive, its secrets waiting to be unraveled.

Raju's grip on reality faltered.

Would he find the truth, or succumb to the darkness?

CHAPTER 22

The Hidden Connection

Raju followed Maya's illusion through the winding streets of Kolkata, the symbols on the walls pulsing brighter with each step. They led him to an ancient temple, hidden behind a waterfall in the heart of the city.

Inside, Raju found a mysterious artifact – a small, ornate box adorned with the same symbols from his apartment.

"This is the key," Maya's illusion whispered. "To unlocking the city's secrets and your own mind."

Raju's hands trembled as he opened the box. A warm light enveloped him, and visions flooded his mind:

Ancient civilizations, long forgotten.
The city's birth, amidst blood and fire.
The secrets hidden within Kolkata's streets.

And his own past, shrouded in mystery.

Raju's mind reeled. The visions were connected to his illness, to the illusions.

Dr. Sen's words echoed in his mind: "Your schizophrenia is a manifestation of your mind's attempt to process the unprocessible."

Raju realized that his illness was not just a curse, but a gateway to understanding the city's hidden language.

CHAPTER 23

The Codebreaker

Raju spent the next few days deciphering the symbols, unlocking the secrets of the artifact. The illusions intensified, but he learned to harness them.

Maya, Kunal, and Kamala appeared, their illusions guiding him through the labyrinthine code.

Together, they uncovered a hidden pattern – a resonance frequency that harmonized the city's energies.

Raju's mind clarified, the fog lifting. He saw Kolkata as a living, breathing entity, pulsing with energy.

The artifact, now a tool, helped him tune into this frequency.

CHAPTER 24

The Harmonizer

Raju stood at the city's center, the artifact in hand. He closed his eyes, focusing on the resonance frequency.

The symbols on the walls began to glow, synchronizing with Raju's heartbeat.

Kolkata's energy began to harmonize, the chaos dissipating.

People stopped, looked around, and smiled. The city's vibrancy returned.

Raju opened his eyes, tears streaming down. He had found his purpose – to maintain the balance, to keep the city's secrets in harmony.

The illusions faded, replaced by a sense of clarity.

Dr. Sen's words echoed once more: "Your mind is capable of extraordinary things, Raju. Embrace it."

Raju smiled, knowing he had found his true self – the codebreaker, the harmonizer, the secret keeper of Kolkata.

Epilogue

Raju's journey transformed him. He continued to explore the city's secrets, using his unique gift to maintain balance.

Maya, Kunal, and Kamala remained close, their bond strengthened by their shared experiences.

Kolkata flourished, its energies in harmony.

And Raju's mind, once a battleground, became a sanctuary – a place where the city's secrets and his own illusions blended into a beautiful symphony.

THE END.

www.ingramcontent.com/pod-product-compliance
Lightning Source LLC
Chambersburg PA
CBHW050024170726
48282CB00025B/535

* 9 7 8 9 3 6 7 8 3 9 6 5 2 *